WILHELM HAUFF

Dwarf Long-Nose

Translated by Doris Orgel

Illustrated by

MAURICE SENDAK

Random House · New York

for ERNA ADELBERG

EARLY in the nineteenth century there lived in Germany a young man named Wilhelm Hauff. Younger than Keats when he died, he left as his legacy to European children dozens of strange and wonderful stories. Among the German-speaking young his name for more than a century has been linked with that of Hans Christian Andersen as a spinner of magical adventures.

For Hauff was that rarity among literary geniuses, an inventor of fairy tales. Few of the great stories—Blue Beard, Rapunzel, Puss-in-Boots—are original fables. Perrault was a collector, as was Lang and as were the Brothers Grimm. There is something about the robust and earthy quality of primitive folktales which seems to defy imitation. That Hauff managed it is a tribute to his odd talent and perhaps only his extreme youth accounts for his ability to create stories as artless and spellbinding as if they had been handed down to him from generations of cottagers.

"Dwarf Long-Nose" remains his most famous tale. It is a story as well-known to children in Germanic countries as "Snow White" or "Sleeping Beauty"; one that for a hundred and thirty years they have begged to have told to them over and over at bedtime. Now in this translation by Doris Orgel, our own children can set out on their first excursions into Wilhelm Hauff's unique and enchanted kingdom.

PHYLLIS McGINLEY

In one of Germany's big cities, many years ago, there lived a righteous, modest shoemaker and his wife. During the day the man would sit on a street corner, mending shoes and slippers, or making new ones if someone would entrust him with the work; but first he had to buy the leather, since he was poor and could keep no supplies on hand. His wife sold fruits and vegetables which she planted in a little garden outside the city gates, and people liked to buy from her, because her appearance was so neat and clean, and because she displayed her wares attractively.

These good people had a handsome son, pleasant of visage, well formed, and rather tall for his twelve years. It was his custom to sit with his mother in the vegetable market, and to help the customers carry their purchases home. He seldom returned from such errands without a beautiful flower, or some money, or a piece of cake, for the fine folk who employed the cooks that bought from his mother liked to have the handsome boy come to their homes and were always generous with their gifts.

One day, the shoemaker's wife was sitting as usual in the market; she had before her some baskets of cabbages and other vegetables, all sorts of herbs and seeds and, in one of the smaller baskets, early pears, apples and apricots. Little Jacob—for this was the boy's name—sat beside her and with his clear voice proclaimed her wares: "Step this way, gentlemen, see the beautiful cabbages and fragrant herbs! New pears, ladies, new apples and apricots! Who will buy? My mother has them all for sale." And as he was calling, an old woman approached; she was ragged and in tatters, had a small, thin face wrinkled with age, red eys, and a pointed, hooked nose which came down almost to her chin. She leaned on a long cane, and it was a wonder that she could walk at all, for she limped and slipped and wobbled; it was as if she had wheels in her legs, and would keel over at any moment, with her pointed nose hitting the pavement.

The shoemaker's wife took a careful look at the old hag. For sixteen years she had sat daily in the market place, and never before had she seen this odd-looking figure. She was startled when the old woman came limping over and stopped in front of her baskets.

"Are you Hannah, the vegetable woman?" the hag inquired in an unpleasant screeching voice, all the while wagging her head to and fro.

.4.

"Yes, I am," the shoemaker's wife replied. "Would you like to buy something?"

"We shall see, we shall see! I'll take a look at your herbs; perhaps you have what I need," replied the old woman as she stooped down over the baskets and with a pair of dark brown, ugly hands examined the one containing the herbs. Disregarding the neat arrangement, she grabbed them with her spider-like fingers and brought them up one by one to her long nose, smelling them this way and that. The shoemaker's wife was revolted to see the hag handling her rare herbs this way; but she dared not say anything, it being the buyer's right to examine the wares, and besides she had a peculiar horror of the woman. When the latter had gone through the entire basket, she mumbled, "Rotten stuff, wretched herbs, nothing at all of what I want; it was much better fifty years ago. Rotten stuff, rotten stuff!"

Her rudeness made little Jacob angry. "See here, you're a shameless old hag," he said. "First you touch the herbs with your hideous brown fingers and squeeze them, then you hold them to your long nose, so that no one who has watched you will want to buy them, then you call our wares rotten stuff when even the Duke's own cook buys from us!"

The hag squinted at the brave little boy, laughed hideously and spoke in a hoarse voice: "Little son,

.6.

little son! So you like my nose, do you, my beautiful long nose? Well, you shall have one, right in the middle of your face, and it shall hang down over your chin, just like mine." And while she spoke she slithered over to the other baskets in which cabbages were displayed. She took the most splendid-looking white heads in her hands, squeezed them so hard you could almost hear them groan, and then threw them back helter-skelter in the basket, saying, "Rotten stuff, rotten cabbages!"

"Don't wobble your head about so!" said the little boy anxiously. "Because your neck is as skinny as a cabbage stem, and could easily break off; then your head would fall into the basket, and who would want to buy that?"

"What, you don't like my thin neck?" the hag mumbled, laughing. "Well then, you shan't have any neck at all! Your head shall stick in your shoulders so that it can't fall off the little body."

"Don't talk such nonsense to the boy," the shoemaker's wife said at last, annoyed with all the probing, squeezing and smelling. "If you want to buy something, then hurry up; you're keeping all my other customers away."

"All right, it will be as you say," the old woman replied with a terrifying look. "I'll buy those six heads of cabbage from you; but look, I have to lean on my

· 7 ·

cane and can't carry anything. Let your little son carry them to my house; I will make it worth his while."

The little one didn't want to go and cried because he was afraid; but his mother urged him to, for she thought it a sin to make the old, weak woman carry such a load. Still crying, Jacob did what she bade him, gathered the cabbages into a cloth, and followed the hag across the market place.

She walked very slowly, but after nearly three quarters of an hour she reached a remote part of the city, where she stopped at last before a small crumbling house. There she pulled an old rusty hook from her pocket, stuck it into a little hole in the door, and suddenly the door sprang open with a loud noise. Imagine little Jacob's amazement when he entered! For the inside of the house was splendidly decorated. The ceilings and walls were of marble, and the furniture, of finest ebony, was inlaid with gold and jewels. The floor was made of glass and so slippery that the little boy tripped and fell several times. After a minute or so the old hag drew a little silver pipe from her pocket on which she blew a tune that was heard all through the house.

Immediately a troop of guinea pigs came marching down the stairs; and Jacob thought them a strange sight indeed. They walked upright on two legs, wearing nutshell shoes on their paws, and fashionable human garb even to hats in the latest style. "What did you do with my slippers, you wretches?" the hag shouted, hitting out at them with her cane so that they jumped in the air and groaned. "How long am I supposed to stand here waiting?"

Quickly they dashed up the stairs and returned with a pair of coconut shells padded with leather inside, which the old woman skillfully put on her feet.

Now, of a sudden, there was no more limping or slipping. She cast aside her cane and glided swiftly over the glass floor, pulling little Jacob along by the

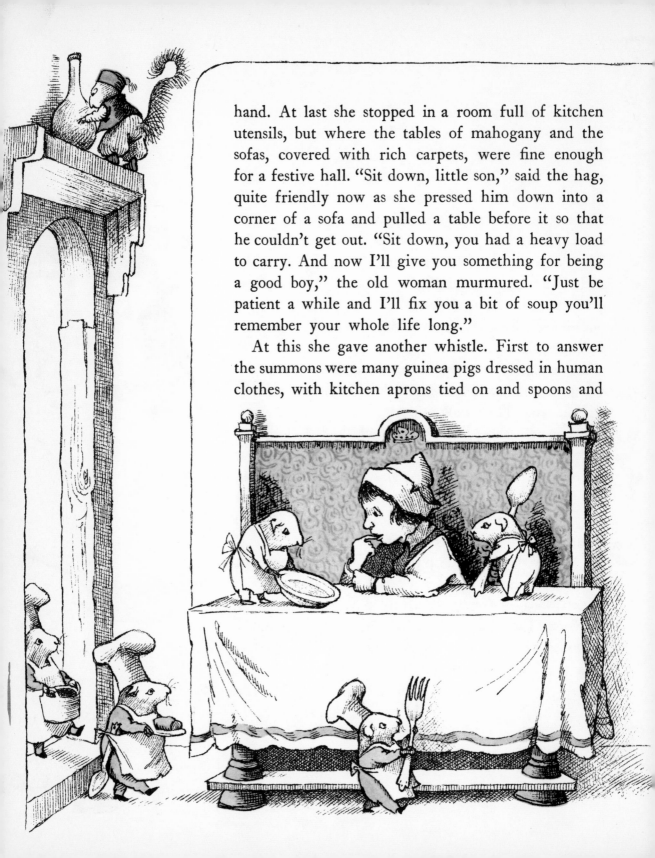

hand. At last she stopped in a room full of kitchen
utensils, but where the tables of mahogany and the
sofas, covered with rich carpets, were fine enough
for a festive hall. "Sit down, little son," said the hag,
quite friendly now as she pressed him down into a
corner of a sofa and pulled a table before it so that
he couldn't get out. "Sit down, you had a heavy load
to carry. And now I'll give you something for being
a good boy," the old woman murmured. "Just be
patient a while and I'll fix you a bit of soup you'll
remember your whole life long."

At this she gave another whistle. First to answer
the summons were many guinea pigs dressed in human
clothes, with kitchen aprons tied on and spoons and

carving knives sticking in their belts. After them a crowd of squirrels came skipping in; these wore wide Turkish pantaloons, walked upright, and had little caps of velvet on their heads. They seemed to be the kitchen boys, for they scrambled with great speed up the walls and brought down pans and bowls, eggs and butter, herbs and flour, and carried them to the stove. There the old woman herself was walking back and forth in her slippers of coconut shell, intent on personally preparing the little boy's soup.

Now the fire was burning high, smoke was coming from the pan, and a pleasant odor pervaded the room; but the hag was still running about with the

squirrels and guinea pigs following, and every time she passed the stove, her long nose bent over the pot. At last it began to bubble and hiss, steam arose from it, and the foam flowed down into the fire. Then she removed the pot from the flames, poured its contents into a silver cup and set it before little Jacob.

"Here, little son, here," she said, "now eat your soup and you shall have all the things you so admired about me! You shall become a skillful cook, too, so that you'll be something in life, but the herb, no, that little herb you'll never find. Why didn't your mother have it in her basket?"

The little boy didn't understand what she was saying; he was paying more attention to his soup, which he found delicious. His mother always prepared good things for him, but nothing had ever tasted quite as good as this. An aroma of fine herbs and spices arose from it; the flavor was both sweet and pungent, and very strong. While he was draining the last drops of the precious stuff, the guinea pigs were burning Arabian incense which was wafting about the room in bluish clouds; the clouds grew ever denser and descended; the smell of the incense made the little boy drowsy; no matter how often he reminded himself that he had to return to his mother, he sank back each time into renewed slumber and finally fell deeply asleep on the old woman's sofa.

.12.

The strangest dream took hold of him there. It seemed to him as though the hag was pulling off his clothes and wrapping him into a squirrel skin. Now he could jump and climb like a squirrel; he joined the other squirrels and guinea pigs, whom he found to be pleasant, well-mannered folk, and began his service in the old woman's employ. At first his only duty was to clean her shoes, which meant having to oil the coconut shells she wore as slippers and rub them till they shone. Since he had often done similar tasks in his father's house, the work went quickly and well. After a year, so his dream continued, he was put to more delicate tasks. He and another squirrel had to catch the little grains of dust in the sunshine, and when they had gathered enough they had to put them through a hair-fine sieve. For the old woman prized this sundust highly, and because she couldn't chew very well, not having a single tooth in her mouth, she had her bread baked from it.

After another year, he was promoted to the rank of those servants who prepared the drinking water for the old woman. This was nothing as commonplace as digging a cistern for the purpose, or catching the rain water in a barrel. No, her method was far more refined: The squirrels, and Jacob with them, had to ladle the dew from roses with hazelnut shells, and that was what the old hag used for drinking water. Moreover, she con-

.13.

sumed it in great quantities, so the water gatherers had much to do.

One more year, and he was transferred to service in the house. Now it was his job to keep the floors clean; and since they were made of glass and showed every breath, this was no slight task. He had to brush them and then polish them, sliding about artfully on them with old rags tied to his feet.

In the fourth year, he was finally promoted to the kitchen. This was an honor, attained only after long trial. Jacob served there from kitchen boy upward to first pastry cook, and acquired such skill and knowledge concerning all things culinary that he was often amazed at himself; the most difficult dishes, pastries with two hundred ingredients, herb soups comprising all the herbs of the world, all these he learned how to prepare with speed and perfection.

Some seven years had gone by when one day the old woman, taking off her coconut slippers and getting her cane and basket in preparation to going out, ordered Jacob to pluck a chicken, fill it with herbs and have it roasted by the time she returned. He did this according to the rules of his art. He killed the chicken, scraped its skin smooth and disemboweled it. Then he began to gather the herbs with which it was to be stuffed.

In the chamber where the herbs were kept he

noticed a little wall cabinet, its door half open, that he had never seen before. Curious, he went closer to see what it contained, and behold, there were many small baskets from which a strong, pleasing odor emanated. He opened one of them and found herbs of the strangest shapes and colors in it. Their stems and leaves were bluish-green and each bore a tiny blossom of burning red mixed with yellow. Thoughtfully he gazed at the flower, smelled it and smelled again that same strong odor which had arisen long ago from the soup the old woman had cooked for him. But the odor was so strong that he began to sneeze, sneezed more and more—and finally woke up, still sneezing.

He was lying on the old hag's sofa and looking around with astonishment. "How very vivid dreams can be," he said to himself. "I could have sworn I was a lowly squirrel, a colleague of guinea pigs and other vermin, and at the same time had become a great cook. How Mother will laugh when I tell her all this! But won't she scold me, too, for going to sleep in a strange house instead of helping her in the market place?"

. 16 .

With these thoughts he got up and prepared to leave. His limbs, he decided, were still stiff from sleeping, particularly his neck, for he couldn't seem to move his head properly; and he had to smile at himself for being so drowsy, because at every moment he was bumping his nose into a wardrobe or the wall, or, turning around quickly, banging it against a doorpost. A squirrel and a guinea pig ran whining about him, as if they wanted to go with him. He asked them to come along when he crossed the threshold, because they were such pleasant little creatures, but they quickly dashed back into the house on their nutshell shoes, and he could still hear them squealing from afar.

It was a very little known part of town where the old woman had led him, and he could hardly find his way out of the narrow streets. Also, a great crowd was gathering; no doubt there was a freak about somewhere near by, because he could hear people calling, "Just look at the ugly dwarf! Where does he come from? See what a long nose he has, and how his head sticks in his shoulders. And look at the brown, ugly hands!" At another time, he probably would have run along with them, because he loved to look at giants, midgets, or people in strange foreign garb; but now he had to hurry to get back to his mother.

He felt somehow odd and fearful when he reached the market place. His mother was sitting there and still had quite a few fruits in her basket, so he couldn't have slept too long. But he could see from a distance that she was very sad; she wasn't calling out to the passers-by, but held her head propped in her hand, and when he came closer, he thought she looked paler than usual. He hesitated, not knowing what to do. At last he took courage, slipped around behind her, trustingly put his hand on her arm, and spoke: "Mother, dear, what's wrong? Are you angry with me?"

The woman turned around to him, but drew back with a cry of alarm:

"What do you want from me, you ugly dwarf?" she exclaimed. "Go away, go away! I don't like such tricks."

"But Mother, what's the matter with you?" Jacob asked, very frightened now. "Surely you are not well; why else would you want to chase your own son away?"

"I told you already, get on your way!" Hannah replied, enraged. "You'll get no money from me with your buffoonery, you ugly monster, you!"

"It must be that God has robbed her of the light of reason!" the little one said to himself, worried, and wondered how he would get her to go home. "Mother, dear," he tried again, "please do be sensible; just look at me; I'm your son, your Jacob!"

"No, now the joke has gone too far," Hannah called over to her neighbor. "Just look at this hideous dwarf! Here he stands, scaring off all my customers, and dares to make sport of my misery. Says to me, I'm your son, your Jacob! How can anyone be so shameless!"

At this the other women got up and began to scold as hard as they could—and market wives, as everyone knows, are good at scolding. They accused him of mocking Hannah in her unhappiness, for seven years ago her handsome son had been stolen from her. They threatened to fall upon him, all together, and scratch him, if he didn't go away at once.

Poor Jacob didn't know what to make of all this. He was certain that he had come to the market with his mother that same morning as every other day, had helped her set up her wares, had then gone to the old hag's house, had tasted a little soup there, slept a little while, and now come back. And yet his mother and her neighbors spoke of seven years! And they called him an ugly dwarf! What was it that had happened to him?

When he saw that his mother didn't want to know him, his eyes filled with tears, and he walked away sadly down the street to the stall where his father mended shoes. "I'll see," he thought to himself, "if he too will not know me; I'll stand under his door and speak with him." When he reached the shoe-

maker's stall, he stood in the doorway and looked in.
The master was so busy working that he didn't see
him; but when he happened to glance toward the
door, he dropped the shoes and shouted with alarm:
"For God's sake, what is that, what is that?"

"Good evening, master!" spoke the little one,
entering the shop. "How goes it with you?"

"Badly, badly, little sir!" the father replied, to
Jacob's great astonishment, for the shoemaker too
seemed not to know him. "The work doesn't go so
easily now. I'm all alone and getting old, but an
apprentice would be too expensive."

"Don't you have a son who could help you by and
by with your work?" the little one asked.

"I had one, his name was Jacob, and by now he

must be a slim, handsome lad of twenty years. He could have been a great help to me. Oh, what a life that would have been! When he was only twelve, he was already handy, and knew a lot about the work, and pleasant and pretty he was, too. He would have attracted lots of customers, and soon I could have stopped mending and only make new shoes! But that's how it is in the world!"

"But where is your son?" Jacob asked his father with trembling voice.

"God only knows," he replied. "Seven years ago, yes, that's how long it's been, he was stolen from us in the market place."

"Seven years ago!" Jacob exclaimed, horrified.

"Yes, little sir, seven years ago; I remember it as though it had happened today, how my wife came home crying and screaming that the child hadn't returned all day. She asked everyone, looked everywhere and couldn't find him. I always thought it was bound to happen, and told her so. Jacob was a handsome child, you had to admit; my wife was proud of him, and liked it when people praised him, so she often sent him to the homes of noble folk with her vegetables and fruit. That was all right; he was always richly rewarded. But take care, I said, this is a large city, there are wicked people here, so take care of our Jacob! And so it happened as I said it would. One day an old, ugly hag came to the market, bargaining for the fruit and vegetables, and buying so much in the end that she couldn't carry it all. My wife, good soul, sent our boy along with her—and hasn't set eyes on him since."

"And that was seven years ago, you say?"

"It will be seven years this spring. We had the town crier call out for him; we went ourselves from house to house and inquired; many people who had known the good-looking boy and grown to like him helped us look, but it was all in vain. No one knew the woman who had bought the vegetables. But an old, old lady who had lived more than ninety years said that it might well have been the wicked fairy of herbs who visits the city once every fifty years to make her purchases."

So spoke Jacob's father, all the while pounding the shoes. And by and by it became clear to the little one what had happened to him. He hadn't dreamed it, but had actually served the evil fairy for seven years as a squirrel. Anger and grief took hold of his heart with such force as to make it want to burst. Seven years of his youth the old hag had stolen from him, and what did he have in return? Knowing how to polish a pair of slippers made of coconuts, or keeping a glass floor clean? Or having learned the secrets of cooking from guinea pigs? He stood there for a long

while thinking about his fate; then at length his father asked him: "Perhaps you want something from me, young sir? A pair of new slippers, maybe, or," he added, laughing, "a leather case for your nose?"

"What is it about my nose?" Jacob asked. "Why should I need a case for it?"

"Well, now," retorted the shoemaker, "each to his own taste! But I must tell you that if I had such a terrible nose, I would have it covered with soft, pink leather. Look, I just happen to have a nice piece here; of course I would need at least a foot of it. But how well it would protect you, young sir! Without it, I'm certain, you bump into every doorpost and into every carriage that you want to avoid."

The little one stood speechless with terror; he felt his nose, and sure enough, it was thick and a good two hand-lengths long! So the hag *had* changed his appearance! That was why his mother hadn't known him, and the people called him an ugly dwarf! "Master," he said, almost weeping now, "don't you have a mirror, that I might look at myself?"

"Young sir," his father replied earnestly, "you don't have the sort of figure that should make you vain, and so you have no cause to look at yourself in the mirror all the time. Give it up; it's a laughable habit, particularly for you."

. 24 .

"Oh, do let me see a mirror," the little one cried out, "and believe me, it isn't for vanity!"

"Leave me alone, I don't own one. My wife has a little mirror, but I don't know where she keeps it. But if you absolutely have to look, well, Urban, the barber, who lives across the street, has a mirror twice as big as your head. You can look in that one, and in the meanwhile, good morning to you."

With these words, his father pushed him gently out of the stall, closed the door behind him and sat down again to his work. The little one, very downcast, went across the street to Urban the barber, whom he remembered well from earlier times. "Good morning, Urban," he said, "I've come to ask a favor of you; be so kind as to let me look into your mirror!"

"With pleasure. There it is," the barber said, laughing, and his customers, who had come to be shaved, laughed with him. "You are a pretty lad, slender and straight, with a neck like a swan's, hands like a queen's, and a tiny little nose as nice as can be. It's true that you're a bit on the vain side; but go ahead and look! No one shall say I didn't let you look because I was envious."

So spoke the barber, and his neighing laughter filled the shop. But the little one had in the meantime stepped before the mirror and seen himself.

. 25 .

"No, dear mother, you could not have known your Jacob again," he said to himself. "This is not what he looked like in the happy days when you liked to show him off to people!" His eyes had become small, like a pig's, his nose was enormous, hanging down over his mouth and chin, and the neck seemed to have disappeared altogether; for his head stuck deep down in his shoulders, and only with the greatest pains could he move it right and left. His body was still the same size as seven years ago when he was twelve years old; but as others grow in height from their twelfth to their twentieth year, so he had grown in breadth; his back and chest were widely distended and looked like a small but heavily filled sack. This thick trunk was supported by small, weak legs which didn't seem up to their burden; all the larger were

. 26 .

the arms hanging from the body, as large as those of a well grown man. His hands were coarse and brownish-yellow, his fingers long and spider-like, and when he stretched them to their full length he could reach down to the floor without bending. That is what he looked like—little Jacob had turned into a misshapen dwarf.

And now he thought of the morning on which the old hag had approached his mother's baskets. Everything he had made fun of at the time—her long nose, the ugly fingers—all this she had passed on to him, as indeed she had said she would, omitting only the long, wobbly neck.

"Well, now, have you looked at yourself long enough, my prince?" said the barber, coming over to him and staring at him with amusement. "Truly, even in the drollest dreams nothing could quite equal your appearance. But I'll make you a proposition, little man. Although my business has always been good, recently it hasn't been quite all it should be. That's because my neighbor, Barber Foam, discovered a giant somewhere who attracts the customers to his shop. Well, growing to giant height isn't so very remarkable; but a little man like you, that's another thing again. Come and work for me, little man. You shall have lodging, food, drink, clothing, everything; in return, you'll stand in my doorway in the morning

. 27 .

and invite the people in. You'll make soapsuds, hand customers the towel, and, rest assured, we'll both stand to profit; I'll get more customers than the other barber with his giant, and they'll all give you a tip, and gladly."

Deep inside, the little one was enraged by the proposition that he be bait for a barber. But then, wouldn't he have to become used to such insults and bear them patiently from now on? He told the barber very calmly that he didn't have time for such employment, and went his way.

The evil old hag may have transformed his body, but she couldn't have stunted his spirit, of that he was sure. For he didn't think and feel any longer as he had seven years ago; no, he believed that in the interval he had grown wiser and more sensible. He didn't mourn over his lost beauty nor over his ugly shape, but only about having been chased away from his father's door like a dog. And so he decided to make one more attempt with his mother.

He went to her in the market place and begged her to listen to him calmly. He reminded her of the day on which he had followed the old woman, recalled to her isolated incidents from his childhood, and then told her how for seven years he served the wicked fairy as a squirrel, and how she changed him because he had mocked her. Everything he told

. 28 .

her about his childhood was as she herself remembered it, but when he spoke of having been a squirrel for seven years, she said: "That is impossible, and there are no fairies," and when she looked at him, she found the ugly dwarf repellent and didn't believe that this could be her son. At last she thought it best to discuss the matter with her husband. So she gathered up her baskets and asked the little one to go with her. Together they went to the shoemaker's stall.

"Look here," she said to her husband, "this person claims to be our lost Jacob. He has told me everything, how he was stolen from us seven years ago, and how a fairy cast a spell on him——"

"Is that so?" the shoemaker interrupted, enraged. "Did he tell you all that? Wait, you scoundrel! I told him the whole story an hour ago myself, and then he goes off to make a fool of you! So the hag cast a spell on you, eh? You just wait, I'll undo the spell soon enough." At this he took a bundle of straps which he had just cut, leaped over to the little one and beat him on his arched back and on his long arms, so that he cried with pain and ran away weeping.

In that city, as anywhere, there were few souls kind enough to help an unfortunate, and fewer still to take pity on someone whose appearance made him laughable. This is how it happened that the poor dwarf went the whole day without food or drink, and at night had to choose the steps of a church, hard and cold as they were, for his resting place.

But the next morning, when the first rays of the sun awoke him, he gave careful thought to how he would earn his livelihood now that his mother and father had rejected him. He was too proud to serve as a barber's display, nor did he want to demean himself by becoming a buffoon and letting himself be viewed for money. What was he to do? Then, all of a sudden, he remembered his culinary training as a squirrel; he thought, not without justification, that with such a background he could hold his own against any cook; and so he decided to make use of this skill.

Therefore, as soon as the streets became livelier and the sun had fully risen, the first thing he did was to enter a church and pray. Then he started out on his way. The Duke, lord of the land, was a well-known gourmet who loved fine cooking and recruited his chefs from all over the world. To his palace the little one went. When he came to the outer portals, the gatekeepers asked him what he wanted and made fun of him; but he asked to see the kitchen master. They laughed and led him through the courtyards, and wherever he passed, the servants would stop, look at him, laugh heartily and follow him so that by and by an enormous procession of all ranks of servants moved up the palace steps. The stableboys threw aside their currycombs, the runners ran as fast as they could, the carpet beaters left their rugs behind, everyone crowded and pushed. There was a tumult as if the enemy stood before the gates, and the air was filled with shouting: "A dwarf! A dwarf! Did you see the dwarf?"

Then the major-domo appeared in the doorway, his face forbidding, an enormous whip in his hand. "You dogs, in Heaven's name, what sort of noise is this? Don't you know that the master is still asleep?"

· 31 ·

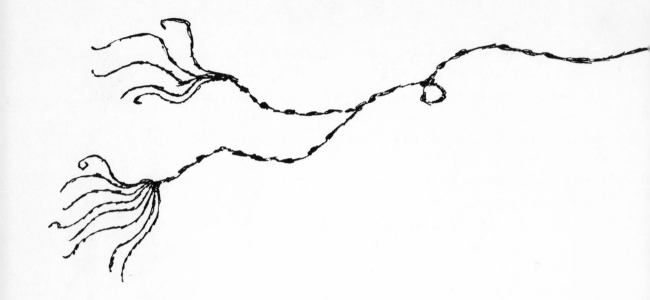

And with this he swung the whip, letting it fall
cruelly on the backs of some stableboys and gatekeepers.

"Oh sir," they called out, "don't you see? We're
bringing a dwarf, a dwarf such as no one has ever
seen before."

The major-domo forced himself not to laugh out
loud when he caught sight of the little one, because
he was afraid that laughing would detract from his
dignity. Instead, he drove the onlookers away with
his whip, led the little one into the house and asked
him what he wanted. When he heard that the dwarf
wished to see the kitchen master, he retorted: "Surely
you've made a mistake; it's me, the major-domo, you

. 32 .

need to see, for you wish to become the Duke's court jester, isn't that so?"

"No, sir," replied the dwarf. "I am an accomplished chef, experienced with all sorts of rare dishes. Take me to the kitchen master; perhaps he can make use of my art."

"Have it your own way, little man; but you're a foolish lad. In the kitchen! As court jester you'd have no work, but all the food, drink and beautiful clothes your heart desires. You couldn't possibly know enough to be the Duke's own chef, and for a kitchen boy you'd be too good, but we shall see." With these words, the major-domo took him by the hand and led him to the kitchen master's quarters.

"Gracious sir," the dwarf said there, bowing so low that his nose touched the rug, "do you have need of an accomplished chef?"

The chief kitchen master inspected him from head to toe, then burst into loud laughter and spoke: "What's that? You, a chef? Do you think our stoves are so low that you could see the top of one even if you stood on tiptoe and worked your head up out of your shoulders? Poor little one! Whoever sent you to me to seek employment as a cook made a fool of you." And he laughed heartily, as did the major-domo and all the servants who happened to be in the room.

.34.

But the dwarf did not allow himself to become discountenanced. "What can an egg or two mean, or a bit of syrup and wine, some flour and spices, in a house where such things are plentiful?" he said. "Give me some delicious dish to prepare, supply me with what I need, and it shall be done quickly, right before your eyes, so you will have to admit that I'm a real chef." Such and similar speeches the little one made, and it was wondrous to watch him, how his eyes sparkled, how his long nose twitched about and his spider's fingers accompanied his words.

"All right, then," said the kitchen master, putting his arm about the major-domo's shoulders. "All right, anything for the sake of a joke. Let's go to the kitchen, then."

They walked through several halls and passageways, and at last arrived at the kitchen. This was a vast and splendidly furnished room; fires burned uninterrupted in twenty stoves; a stream of clear water, in which fish were kept, flowed down the middle; implements that had to be always at hand were kept in cabinets of marble and costly wood; and to the left and right there were ten larders in which were stored whatever had been invented, both in Europe and the East, for the delight of the palate. All sorts of kitchen servants ran about, rattling pots and pans, forks and spoons; but when the chief kitchen master

. 35 .

came in, they all stood still; only the crackling of the fire could be heard and the murmuring of the fresh-water stream.

"What did the master order for his breakfast today?" the chief kitchen master asked the first breakfast maker, a very aged cook.

"Sir, he was pleased to order the Danish soup, and red Hamburger dumplings."

"Good." The kitchen master went on, "Did you hear what the master has called for? Do you dare to prepare these difficult dishes? The little dumplings you can't possibly manage, for the recipe is a secret."

"Nothing easier in the world," replied the dwarf, to everyone's surprise. "Nothing easier!" he repeated, for he had often prepared these dishes as a squirrel. "Let me have such and such herbs for the soup, such and such spices, the fat of a boar, roots and eggs. But for the little dumplings," he lowered his voice so that only the kitchen master and the breakfast maker could hear, "for those I need four sorts of meat, a little wine, duck fat, ginger, and a certain herb called stomach's consolation."

"Holy Saint Benedict! From what magician did you learn this?" the breakfast maker exclaimed with great astonishment. "You have named everything exactly, and even we ourselves didn't know about the

herb called stomach's consolation. Yes, that must make it even tastier. Oh, you marvel of a chef!"

"I would never have thought it," said the chief kitchen master, "but let the test begin! Give him what he requires, dishes and all, and let him prepare the breakfast!"

His orders were carried out, and everything was prepared on the stove. But then it turned out that the dwarf could barely reach up to it with his nose. Therefore a pair of chairs were moved together, a slab of marble was placed over them, and the little wonder man was invited to begin his masterpiece. All the cooks, kitchen boys, servants and other folk stood about in a great circle, watching and marveling

at his skill and speed. When he had done with his preparations, he ordered both dishes to be put on the fire. Then he began to count, one, two, three and so on, and when he reached five hundred, he cried: "Stop!" The pots were taken off, and the little one invited the kitchen master to sample their contents.

The ducal cook had one of the kitchen boys fetch him a golden spoon, rinsed it and handed it to the head kitchen master, who went to the stove with solemn mien, tasted, closed his eyes, smacked his tongue with pleasure and then said, "Superb, by the Duke's own life, superb! Major-domo, wouldn't you also like to taste a little spoonful?" That dignitary bowed down, took the spoon, tasted, and was beside

himself with pleasure and delight. "With due respect for your art, dear breakfast maker, you are an experienced cook; but you have never been able to make either the soup or the dumplings so very delicious." The cook also tasted now, respectfully shook the dwarf's hand and said, "Little one, you are indeed master of your art. Yes, the herb that you have added gives it all a wonderful zest."

At this moment one of the Duke's personal servants entered the kitchen and reported that the master was demanding his breakfast. So the dishes were placed on silver platters and sent in to the Duke. The chief kitchen master took the little one into his room then and chatted with him, but in half the time it would

take to say the Lord's Prayer, a messenger came in to summon the kitchen master to the Duke. Quickly he put on his ceremonial clothes and followed the messenger.

The Duke looked very pleased. He had eaten the entire contents of the silver platters and was just wiping his beard as the head kitchen master came in. "Listen, kitchen master," he said, "I have always been very satisfied with your cooks; but tell me, who prepared my breakfast today? In all the days I have been sitting on the throne of my fathers, I have never tasted anything so delicious. Tell me the cook's name, so that we can give him a present of some ducats."

"Sir, that is a wondrous tale," answered the head kitchen master, and told him how a dwarf had been brought to him that morning who claimed absolutely to be a chef, and how everything had come about. The Duke was greatly astonished. He had the dwarf called before him and questioned him about who he was and where he came from. Naturally poor Jacob couldn't say that a spell had been put upon him and that he had formerly served as a squirrel; still, he stuck to the truth in that he described himself as without father and mother now, and said he had learned to cook from an old woman. The Duke didn't question him further, but amused himself with the odd appearance of his new chef.

. **40** .

"If you will stay with me," he said, "I will give you fifty ducats a year, a suit of festive clothes, and two pair of trousers to boot. But in return, you must personally prepare my breakfast every day, give directions as to the preparation of the noonday meal, and generally occupy yourself with my kitchen. Since everyone in my palace receives his name from me personally, yours shall be Long-Nose, and you shall have the rank of second kitchen master."

Dwarf Long-Nose prostrated himself before the mighty Duke, kissed his feet, and promised to serve him faithfully.

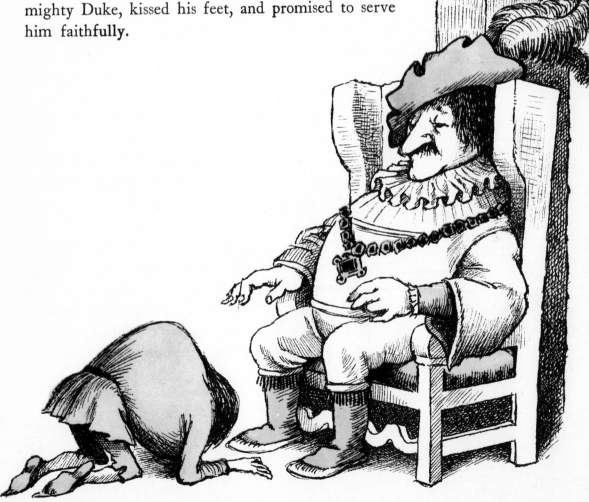

So the little one's immediate worries were over, and he did honor to his office. As for the Duke, one can say in all truth that he was a totally changed man from the day Dwarf Long-Nose came to live in his house. Before, he had been known to throw dishes or platters at the heads of the cooks; yes, the kitchen master himself had had to spend three days in bed once because the Duke had thrown an imperfectly baked leg of veal in his face with great vigor. True, he would try to make amends for his wrath with a few handfuls of ducats; nonetheless, no cook had ever brought his dishes before him without trembling and misgivings. Since the dwarf's arrival, all this had changed, as if by a miracle. Instead of eating three times a day, the Duke ate five times now, in order to do full justice to the art of his little servant; and yet never once did displeasure appear on his face. No, he found everything new and excellent, was gregarious and pleasant, and grew fatter every day.

Often he would summon the kitchen master and Dwarf Long-Nose right in the middle of a meal, seat them to his right and left, and with his own fingers push a few bites of the precious dishes into their mouths, a favor which they both knew how to prize.

The dwarf became the marvel of the city. People would beg the head kitchen master for permission to watch him cook, and a few of the noblest gentry managed to get the Duke to allow their chefs to receive instruction from the dwarf, which brought in not a little money, for each of them paid half a ducat a day. And in order to keep the other cooks in good humor and to prevent their feeling envious, Long-Nose let them have this money which the gentlefolk paid for their chefs' tuition.

Dwarf Long-Nose spent two years this way, living in the greatest comfort and honor, and only the thought of his parents made him sad. And nothing remarkable happened until the following event took place: Being particularly skilled when it came to marketing, the dwarf himself went shopping for kitchen supplies as often as time permitted. One morning, he was on his way to the goose market, looking for the heavy fat ones that his master loved. He had walked up and down several times already, mustering the fowl. Far from causing laughter and mockery now, his form inspired respect, for he was recognized as the famous chef to the Duke, and every market wife with geese to sell was pleased when he turned his nose in her direction.

He happened to see, at the end of a row, a woman sitting in a corner who also had geese to sell, but who wasn't proclaiming her wares and calling after customers. He went over to her and measured and weighed her geese. They were just what he required, and he bought three together with the cage, loaded them on his broad shoulders and began his way back. It struck him as odd that only two of the geese were chattering and shrieking in the manner of their kind, while the third sat quite still and thoughtful, sighing and moaning like a human being. "That one is half

sick," he said to himself. "I'll have to kill her quickly and cook her." But the goose replied quite loudly and distinctly:

> *If you use the knife on me,*
> *I will bite you cruelly.*
> *If you take away my breath,*
> *I'll bring you to an early death.*

Startled, Dwarf Long-Nose set the cage down. The goose looked at him with beautiful, wise eyes, and sighed. "For Heaven's sake," Long-Nose exclaimed, "so you can talk, Miss Goose? I would never have thought so. Well, don't be afraid. Far be it from me to hurt such a rare bird as you. But I'll wager you haven't always worn these feathers. I myself was once a lowly squirrel."

"You're quite right," replied the goose, "when you say that I wasn't born in this wretched shape. Alas, no one predicted at my cradle that Mimi, daughter

of the mighty magician Weatherbuck, would be slaughtered in a Duke's kitchen."

"Calm yourself, my dear Miss Mimi," the dwarf comforted her. "As I am an honest fellow and second kitchen master to his Grace, no one shall harm you. I will prepare a stall for you in my own quarters, you shall have enough to eat, and I will devote my free time to your entertainment. To the other kitchen folk I'll say that I'm fattening up a goose for the Duke with all sorts of special herbs, and as soon as an opportunity presents itself, I'll set you free."

The goose thanked him with tears in her eyes, and the dwarf did as he had promised. He slaughtered the two other geese, but for Mimi he built a special stall under the pretext of preparing her in a special way for the Duke. Nor did he give her ordinary goose fodder, but supplied her with pastries and sweetmeats. As often as he was free, he went to talk to her and comfort her. They told each other their life histories, and Long-Nose heard more about her father, the magician, who lived on a distant island. Once, long ago, this Weatherbuck had quarreled with an old fairy who, with guile and deceitfulness, had got the better of him. Her revenge had been to turn Mimi into a goose and bring her far from home to this place.

When Dwarf Long-Nose had in turn told the goose his story, she said, "I am not inexperienced in

these matters. My father instructed my sisters and me, and told us as much about magic as he was allowed to divulge. The tale of the quarrel at the herb basket, your sudden transformation when you smelled the herb, as well as the few words you say the old woman spoke, are proof to me that you are herb-enchanted, which means that if you find the same herb the fairy had in mind when she cast the spell on you, you can be freed." This was small comfort for the little one; for where was he to find that rare, mysterious herb? Nevertheless, he thanked her and took some measure of hope from what she said.

About this time, the Duke received a visit from a neighboring prince, his friend. Therefore he summoned Dwarf Long-Nose and said to him: "Now the time has come when you must show me whether or not you serve me faithfully, and are truly master of your art. This prince who is to be my guest is known to have the best kitchen next to mine. He is a great connoisseur of fine cooking, and a wise man. Now see to it that you supply my table in such a way as to increase his amazement from day to day. At the risk of my displeasure, don't serve any dish twice as long as he is here. You can ask my treasurer for anything

you need. And even if you must bake gold and dia-
monds in the lard, go right ahead! I would rather
be reduced to poverty than blush before my friend."

The dwarf replied, all the while bowing low, "It
shall be as you wish, sir! I shall do everything in my
power to please this prince of gourmets."

The little chef began then to make use of all his
arts. He didn't spare his master's funds, and spared
himself even less. He could be seen enveloped in a
cloud of smoke and fire all day long, and his voice
resounded through the spacious kitchen as he gave
orders to his underlings, the kitchen boys and lesser
cooks.

Fourteen days of the foreign prince's visit went

by, and he enjoyed himself greatly. He and the Duke ate together every day, no less than five times, and the Duke was well pleased with the art of his dwarf, for he saw contentment on the face of his guest. But on the fifteenth day it happened that the Duke had Long-Nose called to the table, introduced him to the prince and asked the latter what he thought of the dwarf.

"You are a wonderful chef," the foreign prince replied, "and know what it means to eat well. In all the time I've been here, you haven't repeated a single dish, and everything has been splendidly prepared. But tell me, why are you delaying so long with the queen of all dishes, a Souzeraine pâté?"

The dwarf was very alarmed, for he had never heard of this best of all pâtés. But he collected himself and replied, "O Sir! I hope your face will grace this court for a long while still, and that is why I was waiting with that dish; for with what else should the chef greet you on the day of your departure but with this queen of pâtés?"

"Is that so?" retorted the Duke, laughing. "And you would have kept me waiting until my death before greeting me thus? Because you've never served me that pâté either. But please think of another parting greeting, for tomorrow you shall serve the Souzeraine."

"It shall be as **you say, sir**," replied **the** dwarf, and **he** left. But he didn't go cheerfully, for the day of **his** shame and misery had come. He simply had no **idea** how to prepare the pâté. So he retired to his room and wept over his fate. Just then the goose, Mimi, who was free to walk about in his quarters, came to him and asked about the cause of his grief.

"Dry your tears," she replied when she had heard about the pâté Souzeraine. "This dish was often served at my father's table, and I know approximately what you need for it; you take this and that, in such and such quantities, and even if that isn't absolutely all that is required, the chances are these gentlemen won't know the difference."

So spoke Mimi. But the dwarf jumped up with

joy, blessed the day he had bought the goose, and set to preparing the queen of all pâtés. First he made a trial portion, and behold, it tasted wonderful, and the chief kitchen master, to whom he gave a sample, once again praised his art.

The next day he prepared a larger quantity of the pâté, and sent it to the table warm, directly from the stove, decorated with wreaths of flowers. He himself put on his most festive clothes and went into the dining room. When he entered, the head server had just cut the pâté and was passing it to the Duke and his guest on a silver serving dish. The Duke took a hearty bite, cast his eyes up to the ceiling and said, after he had swallowed: "Ah! Ah! Ah! This is quite rightfully called queen of pâtés; but then my dwarf is the king of all chefs! Isn't that so, dear friend?"

The guest took a few small bites, tasted and examined them carefully, all the while smiling in a mocking and mysterious way. "The thing is artfully prepared," he answered, pushing his plate aside, "but it isn't altogether the Souzeraine—just as I expected."

The Duke wrinkled his brow with displeasure and blushed with shame. "Dog of a dwarf!" he shouted. "How dare you do this to your master? Should I have your big head chopped off in punishment for your bad cooking?"

"O Sir, in Heaven's name, didn't I prepare the dish according to the rules of the art? Surely there can be nothing wrong!" So spoke the dwarf and he trembled.

"That's a lie, you scoundrel!" the Duke replied, and kicked him away with his foot. "Or my guest wouldn't say that there was something missing. I'll have *you* chopped up and baked in a pâté next!"

"Have mercy!" the little one cried, sliding on his knees toward the guest and clasping his feet. "Tell me, what does this dish lack that it doesn't please your palate? Don't let me die because of a handful of meat and flour."

"That won't help you much, my dear Long-Nose," the stranger replied, laughing. "I suspected yesterday that you couldn't make this dish as well as my own chef. All right, then, I'll tell you: A special herb is missing, that isn't even known in these parts—the herb Sneezewithease. Without it the pâté lacks all zest, and your master will never know its real taste as I do."

This infuriated the Duke. "Know it I *will*!" he exclaimed with glittering eyes. "For I swear it on my ducal honor; either the pâté as you know it is served us tomorrow, or this fellow's head shall be fixed to my palace gate. Go now, you dog. I grant you yet another twenty-four hours' grace."

. 54 .

Again the dwarf went weeping to his room, and bemoaned his fate to the goose, crying that he must die; for he had never heard of the herb.

"If it's only that," she said, "then I can help you; for my father taught me to know all herbs. At any other time of the month it would have looked bad for you, but luckily we have a new moon now, and it is then that the herb is in bloom. But tell me, are there any old chestnut trees in the vicinity of the palace?"

"O yes!" Long-Nose replied, the burden on his heart growing lighter. "Down by the lake, two hundred paces from the house, there is a whole group of them. But why do you ask?"

"Only at the foot of an old chestnut tree does this herb bloom," said Mimi. "So let us not lose any time, but look for what you need; take me on your arm and put me down outside; I will search for you."

He did as she said, and went with her to the palace gate. But there the gatekeeper, gun in hand, said, "My dear Long-Nose, for you everything is over. I have the strictest orders not to allow you out of the house."

"But surely I can go in the garden?" retorted the dwarf. "Be so good as to send one of your colleagues to the major-domo and ask whether I can't go in the garden to look for herbs."

The gatekeeper did so, and permission was granted; for the garden was surrounded by high walls, and escape from it was impossible. So when Long-Nose had passed the gate with Mimi, he set her down gently, and quickly she preceded him to the lake, down to where the chestnut trees stood. He followed her with troubled heart, for it was his last and only hope. If she didn't find the herb, he would throw himself into the lake then and there rather than let himself be beheaded.

But search as she might, the goose searched in vain; she looked under every chestnut tree, she turned every blade of grass about with her beak; still there was no sign of the herb, and she began to cry in pity and fear; for night was beginning to fall and the objects around were becoming more difficult to recognize.

Just then the dwarf's glance fell across the lake, and suddenly he called out: "Look, look, there across the lake stands still another big old tree; let's go there and look, perhaps my luck will blossom yet!"

The goose hopped excitedly and flew ahead, Long-Nose running after her as fast as his little legs would carry him. The chestnut tree cast a large shadow, and it was dark all around and well nigh impossible to see; but all of a sudden the goose stood still, beat her wings with joy, then quickly submerged her head

in the high grass and picked up something which she handed daintily with her beak to the astonished Long-Nose, saying as she did so: "This is the herb, and there's a lot of it growing here, so you can have all you need."

The dwarf gazed thoughtfully at the little plant. The same sweet odor he had smelled on the day of his transformation was wafting towards him now, and he recognized the stem and leaves of bluish-green, and the flaming red blossom with the yellow border.

"Praised be God!" he called out at last. "What a miracle! Because I believe it was the very same herb that caused my transformation into this miserable shape. Should I try the experiment?"

"Not yet," begged the goose. "First take a handful of the herb and let us go to your room and gather your possessions. Then we'll test the strength of the herb."

Long-Nose agreed, and went back to his room with her, his heart beating audibly with expectation. When he had made a bundle of his clothes, shoes, and the fifty or sixty ducats he had saved up, he spoke: "So please it God, I'll be rid of this burden now." And he sank his nose deep into the herbs and inhaled their fragrance.

Immediately he felt a cracking and pulling in all his joints. His head was lifting itself out of his

. 58 .

shoulders, and as he peered down on his nose he saw it grow smaller and smaller. His back and chest began to even out, and his legs grew longer.

Great was the goose's wonder as she watched all this. "Oh! How tall, how handsome you are!" she exclaimed. "God be praised, there's nothing of the dwarf left in you!"

Jacob was so overjoyed at this that he folded his hands and prayed. But his joy didn't let him forget the thanks he owed the goose Mimi. Although his heart urged him to hurry to his parents, his gratitude conquered this wish and he spoke: "Whom else but you have I to thank for receiving my own self back? I never would have found this herb without you, and would have had to remain in that awful shape forever, or else die under the henchman's axe. Well now, I will repay you. I will take you home to your father; surely he, who is so well versed in every spell, will know how to free you from the one that holds you captive."

The goose shed tears of joy and accepted his offer. Jacob passed the palace gates with her unrecognized, and began his way toward the seashore and Mimi's home.

They brought their journey to a happy conclusion. The magician Weatherbuck freed his daughter from the spell, and, after giving Jacob lavish presents, bade him a fond farewell. Jacob returned to his native land where his parents joyfully recognized the handsome youth as their son, and with Weatherbuck's gifts he bought a store which brought him riches and happiness.

But in the palace there was a great commotion after his departure; for the next day, when the Duke

wanted to carry out his oath and have the dwarf beheaded if he hadn't found the herbs, the dwarf was nowhere to be found. The prince claimed that the Duke had secretly helped the dwarf to escape so as not to deprive himself of his best cook, and accused him of being untrue to his word. Out of this arose a great war between the two rulers which is well known in history as the "War of Herbs." Many a battle was fought, but in the end peace was concluded, a peace which is referred to as the "Pâté Peace," because at the feast of reconciliation the prince's chef prepared the queenly Souzeraine with which the Duke delighted his palate.